A Hare's Tale

Rob Auty

R. Auty

Illustrations by
Chaz Wood
www.chaz-wood.com

2QT Limited (Publishing)

First Edition published 2011 by
2QT Limited (Publishing)
Dalton Lane, Burton In Kendal
Cumbria LA6 1NJ

Cover Design by Robbie Associates
Cover Images supplied by istockphoto.com
Typesetting by Dale Rennard

Also Available as a eBook Kindle (without illustrations)
ISBN: 978-1-908098-27-6

Printed in Great Britain
Lightning Source UK Ltd

A CIP catalogue record for this book is available
from the British Library
ISBN 978-1-908098-25-2

Prologue
A Hare in the Garden

Patrick stroked the head of the wooden statue in the walled garden, "Nice bunny," he said quietly.

His mother watched him and smiled as the memories flooded back. She remembered buying the statue from the 'Bodger' at the side of some road or other several years earlier.

'It's cherry wood, you only need to oil it a couple of times a year to keep it in good condition, Ma'am', the Bodger had said.

The 'Cherry Wood' Hare

It hadn't really mattered what wood it was made of, or how much it had cost, Samantha, the little boy's mother, would have bought it no matter what, because it reminded her of the little Hare she'd met all those years before.

"It isn't a bunny, Patrick, it's a Hare, they are very different animals you know," she told her son.

"It looks like a bunny, Mummy, it's the same as the bunnies that run around the garden in the mornings," Patrick said, quite importantly.

"Well it isn't a bunny, Darling, it is a Hare. I know a lot about them, and I met one once, when I was a little girl."

"You met one?" Patrick looked at her with one eyebrow raised, "Tell me the story, Mummy!" he said excitedly.

Samantha smiled to herself and then got up off the comfortable garden seat she'd been sitting on, "Wait here, Darling, I'm going in the house for just a minute or two," she told Patrick.

Patrick smiled at her and sat down next to the Hare, it was bigger than him in that position, and the picture created gave Samantha a very comfortable feeling. She waved and smiled and entered the house.

She went upstairs and into her bedroom and searched under the bed until she pulled out a dusty old suitcase that she then placed on the bed. She opened the latches and blew away some dust and rummaged inside the case until she found what she wanted, a pile of old, slightly yellowed paper.

She smiled at the memory again: her parents had indulged her at the time. She looked at the top sheet, 'A Hare's Tale' was the only thing written on the first page. She shook her head slightly at the thought of the hours she'd spent writing this story as a young girl, her imagination fired by the strange events of that lovely March day all those years ago.

She took the manuscript down to the garden

and seated herself on the chair once more, "Come over here, Patrick, and I'll tell you the story of Juney Brown Toes, a Hare I once... knew."

Patrick joined her on the wide chair and wriggled until he was comfortable.

"Are we sitting comfortably," She asked her son, he laughed out loud, it was their little ritual and joke before every story-time.

"Yes!" shouted Patrick.

"Then let's begin," said Samantha.

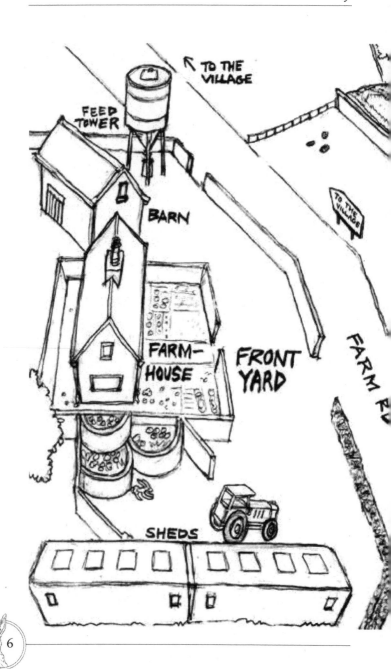

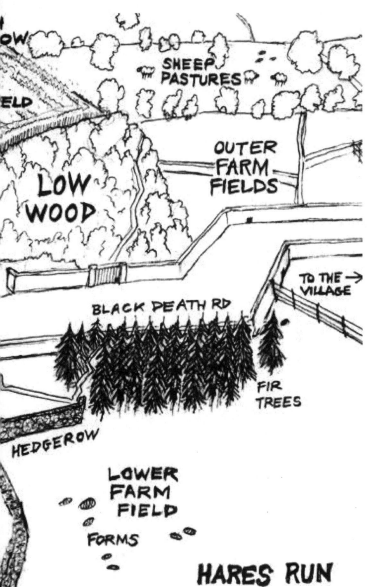

Chapter One
A Hare's Breadth

Juney Brown Toes sat and listened to her teacher, Wimble Whitecoat. He was an impossibly old Hare. He had lived as long as seven summers, and for a Hare that was very old indeed.

Juney was an above average Hare, for a Doe, she was tall, and had rich golden brown fur, long sleek ears with black tips, and her toes were all a deep rich dark brown colour, hence her name, Juney Brown Toes. Her eyes were unusual too, for a Hare, dazzling blue in colour.

Juney Brown Toes

The other Hares in the class were Jacks and they weren't paying much attention to Wimble, but that was the nature of the Jacks, boy Hares, they tended to be flighty, to run at the mildest of noises and to fight the night away, when they should be eating and learning.

Tufty Thomas, one of Juney's friends, was a tall and skinny Jack, he was named for the great tuft of hair between his wonderfully long ears. He and several of the other Jacks were teasing poor Slow Freddy, named because in every Hare race he competed in, and there were many, he usually finished last. Freddy had a yearning for mushrooms, as many as he could find and eat, and that made him rather large for a Hare. Some unkind Hares even suggested that Freddy might be fat!

Juney listened to Wimble's voice and stared at the moonlit night sky. She loved the nighttimes when a Hare could enjoy herself in the darkness, running, playing and eating, while most of their enemies slept. Men and foxes were the main ones, men didn't trouble them at night on the whole, but Mr Fox could be troublesome, sneaking up on you and pouncing, and before you knew were you where you'd be fox dinner!

Juney shook the thought from her head. She was fast! And she had keen senses. No one would ever catch Juney. During the day she would dig her Form, a Hare bed, and settle down in it, ears flat, quiet and invisible deep in the grass. Stillness and speed were the defences of a Hare, and Juney was a master of both.

By now, at a year old, she should have had her first Leverets, baby Hares, but Juney didn't want to be tied down, she loved to run and play with the Jacks. The other Doe's looked down on her as they busied themselves gathering food and taking care of their Leverets. "She'll be to old, before long," and, "shameful!" were comments often whispered behind her back.

Apart from ancients like Wimble Whitecoat, the legendary Golden Hare, and the mysterious Blueback, Hares tended not to live overlong. Mr Stoat, Owls, Hawks, and Mr Fox took Leverets regularly, and even Buck rabbits, which are Daddy rabbits, would kill Leverets if they found them! And when finally a Hare was grown enough and could outrun most of these menaces, men would bring their dogs, and the Hares would face new dangers.

Even dogs and men could be outrun sometimes, unless the evil 'Grey Hound' was present. Here was a terrifying beast, whose name was used by mother Doe's to frighten naughty Leverets. A dog that could run faster than a Hare for a short time, dangerous! But so far a Grey Hound had never challenged Juney. She was a lucky Hare.

Her attention was drawn back to her lesson. Wimble was recounting the story of Blueback and the Eagle. It was a wondrous story of how

Blueback had cheated the Eagle and saved himself at the expense of a Grey Hound and its Man owner. Juney listened avidly even though she had heard the story many times, but the Jacks were becoming boisterous, and Freddy was their focus.

Wimble stopped telling his story and intervened on Freddy's behalf, "A- Hare's -breadth, -should -not, -and -does -not —matter, -leave —Freddy — alone," he said in his deep and deliberate voice, "-you —boys —would —do —well —to —look —to — your —lessons —and —leave —Freddy —alone!"

That was enough for the Jacks, Wimble was well respected amongst the Hare's and his word was final. The boys settled down into the school Forms and, ears erect, concentrated on Wimble's stories.

Wimble Whitecoat tells the Jacks to behave

Chapter Two
Mad as a March Hare

"Lepus' ghost, it's a cold morning," Freddy said. He and several other Jacks milled around the cornfield, generally acting the fool and practising their boxing skills.

It was cold with a fresh bright sunlit sky, on a beautiful March morning, and Juney played with the Jacks. She stopped playing to tell Freddy off, "Freddy do not use Lepus' name like that. He is the Lord of Hares, and one day you may need his help!"

Freddy dropped his head, "I'm sorry, Juney, but it *is* cold!" he said.

"Then practise your boxing, here, I'll box with you," she stood on her hind legs and swung her front feet playfully at Freddy.

Freddy lifted himself lazily off the ground, and swayed unsteadily, his great bulk threatening to knock him over before he could throw a punch. And that's exactly what happened, he fell over as he attempted to box, and landed heavily on a cornhusk, "ouch!" he cried.

"Oh, Freddy," said Juney, "you are really going to have to exercise more and eat less mushrooms. If Mr Fox gets you he'll think his all his birthdays have come at once!" she couldn't help herself and she laughed.

"But I like mushrooms!" Freddy moaned.

"Let's go up to High Meadow and practise the Runs, we can race!" one of the Jacks suggested in a loud voice.

"Are you sure?" Tufty asked, "Hawk and maybe even Eagle will be about on a clear day like today," he said in his quiet and squeaky voice.

"So what! We are Jacks, and it is March, it's time to be mad!" said the loud Jack, and he turned and disappeared amongst the closely planted corn stalks. One by one the Jacks followed, until only Juney, Freddy and Tufty remained.

"Well I'm not a Jack, and I'm not mad, but if they want to race I'm up for it!" said Juney, and she ran after the Jacks.

"Oh dear," was all Tufty said as he followed Juney.

"Ohhh, wait for me!" wailed Freddy and he waddled after them.

After a few minutes the Jacks and Juney arrived at High Meadow, long green and golden grass greeted them as far as the eye could see.

"Right," said the loud Jack, "get to your starting Form's and no cheating!"

The Hares spread out across the meadow. Hares spent a lot of time practising escaping from things that wanted to kill and eat them. And so every Hare prepared a 'Run', an escape route, practised every day until a Hare could run it with its eyes closed. Each 'Run' had a Form in several different locations.

This particular race, it was decided, would start in High Meadow, and finish down in the lower farm field Form, where you could actually see the farmhouse! *The Jacks are particularly mad this morning!* Thought Juney, but she was a game Hare and wouldn't back out.

Juney settled into her High Meadow Form and waited for the start. She saw Marty Lop Ear sneaking forward. Marty had a broken ear, damaged in a tussle with an angry stoat, and he was currently well forward of his Form. "Cheater!" Juney yelled, but she held her own position and waited for the start.

Marty looked back at her and stuck his tongue out and then he turned and, ignoring her angry and indignant squeals, shuffled further forward.

Marty Lop Ear being cheeky!

"Ready," shouted the loud voiced Jack, "Steady! Go!"

And they were off. Juney raced away, flying over her run. Passing Marty, who's run briefly intersected hers, she raced away from the startled Jack.

A Hare's run was never a straight run. Yes there were some long straight sections where a Hare could gather speed, but as well, there were frequent twists and turns to 'Out Fox' whomever was chasing them, and to confuse the scent their enemies were following. Juney hurtled down and out of High Meadow, and into the first of the sheep pastures, here she opened up and

Juney Brown Toes in full flight

all but flew past the startled sheep. A Hare can run as fast as forty miles an hour at times, and the sight of several Hares running like lightening across their field, sent the sheep hither and thither from one corner of the field to the other, not knowing which way to turn.

Juney was first back to the cornfield where, normally, Hares would zigzag, confusing the ones who wanted to eat them, but Juney was different

to most Hares. She was daring and she was fast, so she simply ran straight through the corn, brushing past stems, and leaping over fallen husks, she burst from the field far ahead of the Jacks.

On she went, through Low Wood, and then into the outer farm fields. She looked back and could just see Tufty, who was nearly as fast as her, and Marty in the distance, just clearing the wood.

She crossed Black Death Road in a flash, entered a copse of fir trees and finally leaped into her Form in the lower farm field. She stood erect, breathing hard, and waited for the others. Normally she would lay flat in her Form during the daylight hours, but she didn't want the Jacks to miss her as they entered the field, she had won again, and they would not be pleased!

Chapter Three
A Hare of the Dog

Tufty was second, and then Marty. The loud Hare, called Harry White Tail, was next, and then the next few came all at once, with Slow Freddy last, a long way behind.

"Oh I need to rest, and I need some food, and my feet hurt!" Freddy moaned.

"If we had a competition for moaning, Freddy, you'd win it every time," Harry said loudly. Harry did everything noisily.

"You won again, Juney!" Tufty said, "will we ever beat you?" he asked good-naturedly.

"One day someone will, I'm sure," Juney replied, "but not for a long time yet!" she laughed and jumped about, generally annoying most of the Jacks.

"You can't win at everything!" Harry shouted.

"Well name your game, Harry White Tail, and we'll see," Juney replied.

Juney had her back to the farm and Harry looked over her shoulder and smiled, *only a Hare can tell when another Hare smiles, by the way,* "I know!" he said, "We'll play 'A Hare of the Dog'," Harry said.

The Jacks were nervous, and Juney turned around. Old Lab, the big dog from the farm had entered the field, he was ambling as fast as his big frame would carry him towards the Hares.

"That's dangerous and silly!" Juney said. Quite a few Hares had met unfortunate ends playing *that* game.

"It's March! And we are Mad March Hares!"

Tufty Thomas

Harry bounced from one great foot to another, "Come on, Jacks, everybody can beat, Juney today!"

With that Harry bounded off towards Old Lab, Bobby Red Eyes and Billy Scar Nose where hot on his heels. Marty and a few of the other Jacks scarpered and disappeared into the woods, leaving, Tufty and Freddy with Juney.

'A Hare of the Dog' had no rules, the bravest of the Hares would get close enough to a dog to nip off a tuft of fur, or pluck a single whisker from their foe. But it was dangerous, very dangerous.

"It's only, Old Lab, Juney," said Tufty, "he couldn't even catch, Freddy."

"I know," Juney replied, "but it's a silly game!" she didn't want to admit she was afraid. Dogs, more than Foxes, frightened her greatly.

"Well I'm going to have a go," said Tufty, and he took off towards the other three Hares who were already teasing Old Lab.

Freddy hides in Juney's Form

"Ohhhh, Freddy, you stay here! Understand?" said Juney.

"No fear, Juney, I'm not going anywhere near a dog," Freddy hunkered down into Juney's Form. Juney raced off to join in the game.

They ran Old Lab ragged, he was a poor old dog, overweight and past his prime, but he still had enough about him to snarl and snap and the Jacks didn't get close enough to him to win the game.

Juney ran straight in from the side of Old Lab, and sped between the dog's legs, grabbing a tuft of hair as she raced under him.

"I win again!" she said, brandishing the hair from a safe distance.

"Oh! Not again!" shouted Harry in disgust.

The hares spy real danger!

Just then Freddy raced past, as fast as his over large body would let him. Juney looked back, "Grey Hound!" she screamed in horror.

She had never seen one before but she instantly knew what it was from Wimble's stories. She took off towards the trees.

Several things happened at once, Harry ran for cover, Tufty ran after Freddy, Bobby backed away, terrified, and ended up in the jaws of Old Lab, and Billy ran directly at the Grey Hound, dodging out of the way at the last instant and racing away to safety.

Bobby backs away, terrified

Interlude

"Wait a minute," Patrick said with a trembling lip, "does that mean Poor Bobby is… dead?"

Patrick asked his mother.

"Sadly yes," Samantha said, stroking a little tear from Patrick's face, "unfortunately Hares have many enemies, eagles, owls, hawks, dogs, and many more, and if they are silly to boot, well… "

"And even Buck Rabbits will kill baby Hares, if they get a chance?" Patrick asked.

"Even Buck Rabbits, yes, Patrick. Do you want me to stop?"

"No, I've got to know what happens!" Patrick said wide-eyed.

"Then, are we sitting comfortably?"

"Yes!" Patrick sat up eagerly.

Chapter Four
A Bad Hare Day

Juney panicked, she ran this way and that for a few seconds, and then calmed down. She spied the Grey Hound, it was arguing with Old Lab over poor Bobby, and she could see Freddy, still in the field, puffing and panting, while good old Tufty encouraged him on to safety.

She began to run towards Freddy, and unfortunately so did the dreadful Grey Hound, it was a sleek and skinny beast, with a long pointed jaw, and it flowed over the ground almost as fast as a Hare in its prime.

36 Juney puts herself in danger to save Freddy

Juney changed direction and ran faster than she had ever done before in her life, flying past the snout of the Hound, and drawing it away from Freddy and Tufty. The beast chased her, she skipped right and left, almost turning full circle at one point, and still it chased.

She bent low to the ground and ran even faster, she felt its hot breath on her haunches and dragged

another effort from her straining muscles, and then it was gone… she turned and slowed down to see the Grey Hound loping off towards Freddy and Tufty, who were by now closing in on the hedgerow.

She chased the Hound. Freddy and Tufty disappeared into the hedge. The Hound followed and a sudden yelping and snarling noise stopped Juney in her tracks. The Hound was stuck under

Grey Hound chases Freddy

the hedge, and she could hear Freddy beyond the hedge, squealing as if Mr Fox had him.

Juney raced around the hedge, and slowly worked her way towards the point the Jacks would have emerged onto Farm Road. Tufty sat in the middle of the road, looking left and right, panicking, as he was sometimes prone to do in a crisis. Juney ran up to him to see what was wrong.

To the left of Tufty, the Grey Hound was stuck in the hedgerow, snarling and snapping, and through the growls, Juney was sure she could hear words, "I'm going to eat fat juicy Hare!". It struggled viciously and Juney gathered all her courage to move closer and see what held the beast. Barbed wire was wrapped around its collar, but every few tugs and snags it released it a little.

Juney turned to Tufty, 'Go, and get help, bring everyone! Everyone who can come!"

Tufty didn't reply, released from his panic by a task he could accomplish, he hurtled away.

Juney ran to the other side of the road and gasped when she saw Freddy. His large rear end stuck out into the road and his head disappeared into the hedge. He moaned and squealed like a Hare already in the jaws of the Hound. He struggled and pulled, but Juney couldn't see where he was trapped, or get an understandable word out of him.

She ran along the hedge until she found a spot she could get under, and then she darted through it. She was in the big front yard of the Farm House, and she stood stock still until she was sure nothing, Hound or Man, was about. The big red thing the Humans sometimes rode in was nowhere to be seen. Juney was an intelligent Hare, and understood the concept of Men getting into things, rather than, as some Hares thought, the big, noisy 'monsters' that used the Roads were actually living beasts. But Juney knew differently, and so when the Farmer's road thing was missing, it told Juney that the People were not likely to be there either.

She hurried up to Freddy, who was still rambling and squealing. Juney noticed that his head was stuck through a flat piece of wood. He must have run straight into it in his panic, she thought. His head had come through, but the rest of him was far too large, and his big ears were preventing him from escaping.

Juney examined the wood he was trapped in, it ran into the hedge for several Hare strides in both directions, and she was at a loss as to what to do.

"Freddy, calm down, and try going backwards, CALM DOWN! The Grey Hound is trapped too," she shouted.

Freddy heard her and said, "Oh dear, Oh dear, I'm having a bad Hare day, today!" but he had listened and was slowly trying to back out of his predicament, unfortunately, as Juney had suspected, his ears prevented him from releasing himself.

"OH DEAR!" Freddy wailed, "I am going to be a Grey Hounds' dinner!"

Freddy is well and truly stuck!

"Stop that at once, Freddy! The Hound is enraged by your noise, you are a Hare in a tight situation, act like one!" Juney said firmly.

Freddy mumbled something, but he became Hare like, quiet and all but invisible.

"Now, Freddy, " Juney whispered, "I am going to get help… from somewhere, stay quiet, and the Hound might give up his struggles as well."

Freddy looked like he wanted to reply, but he remained silent, and Juney moved quietly away, following the hedge until she found a way through. Back on the Road, she made sure that the Hound did not see her and she lay a long ear on the black surface to listen.

A Hare has incredible hearing, and Juney listened to hear if anything was near that could help poor Freddy.

A vibration caught her attention and she looked up again, glancing down the Road, a machine was coming, it was far off but it was coming. An outrageous idea began to form in Juney's mind. It was against all

Hare instincts to seek help from anyone or anything other that another Hare. But she had watched the Farmer on occasion and he seemed a gentle sort, he had seen her and other Hares and had never made a threatening move or gesture towards them.

Juney decided she would do it! She would seek the aid of whoever was coming along the Road! She ran in the direction of the vibration, straight down the middle of the road.

Chapter Five
Running with the Hare

The Farmer drove his old red car down the Farm Road. He had just picked up his wife and two children from the local village fair.

"Not too fast, Charlie," his wife said.

"Only doing thirty miles an hour, Mother," he replied.

"Watch where you're going, dear," his wife added.

The Farmer tutted and muttered under his breath.

"What was that?" Mother shouted.

"Err, nothing, dear," replied the farmer.

"No," she said what was that?" she pointed out the back window of the car.

The farmer slowed and looked in his rear-view mirror, "Don't rightly know, love, looks like a rabbit, a big one though," he said.

"It's a Hare! And a beautiful one," Samantha, the Farmers daughter shouted in excitement from the backseat, "I've seen pictures at school," she added.

Her brother, Adam, got up on his knees and pushed his face up to the rear window, "It's following us, Pa," he said.

"Well it won't be for long," said the Farmer, and he pressed the accelerator and drove off at speed.

Juney watched the red thing pull away with Farmer inside it and she gave chase, she soon caught up and, when the road widened, she ran straight past the car and kept running until she was some distance ahead, there she waited.

"Well that is bizarre," the Farmer said, scratching his chin as he slowed the car down to stop about ten feet from the Hare.

"Run it over, Pa, we can have it for supper!" Adam suggested enthusiastically.

"NO! DON'T YOU DARE!" Samantha screeched as she dragged her brother back onto the rear seat and took his place between the front seats.

"She's gorgeous, look at those lovely blue eyes!" she said, pointing.

"How do you know it's a she?" Adam asked, slumped back in his seat he knew better than to argue with Samantha when she was in this mood, his sister was smaller, but he knew better.

Interlude

"That's you, Mummy!" Patrick said, interrupting the story.

"Yes, Darling, it's me, your Uncle Adam, Granny, and Gramps," Samantha replied.

"Then it's all true?" Patrick asked.

"Well, everything from here on is true, well everything when I'm in the story, the stuff before, and the bits after, I wrote after we met, Juney."

"How do you know her name, could she talk?" Patrick was puzzled.

"I gave her the name, and the others...

but maybe I should finish the story first?" she suggested.

"Yes!" Patrick said.

"Look at her! I just know," Samantha said firmly. She pushed Adam aside and started to get out of the car.

"Where do you think you are going, young lady," her mother asked.

"She's obviously waiting for us, I'm going to see what she wants," Samantha said matter-of-factly.

"Stay in the car! It might be dangerous!"

"Mother, it's a Hare, what's she going to do? Eat me?" Samantha asked in that condescending way only children can do.

Her Mother's mouth opened once or twice, and she looked indignant. Then she just shook her head and said, "Oh get on with it, I've got tea to do, and we haven't got all day."

Samantha got out of the car and slowly walked towards the Hare. It stood stock still until Samantha was within three feet of it, and then it took a step away. Samantha stopped, "Hey there, my name is, Sam," she told the Hare, she much preferred Sam, but her family still insisted on Samantha, all except Pa, when no one else was about.

The Hare hopped a few feet further down the road and stopped to look directly at Sam.

"You want me to follow?" Sam stepped forward as she spoke, and the Hare moved again. Sam turned around and gestured to her Pa to follow.

The Hare moved off slowly and Sam began to jog down the road after it, it picked up speed and so did Sam. The Farm was only a few hundred yards further on, and Sam began to run, the Hare took off, occasionally looking back to make sure Sam was following.

She was running with the Hare and she found it exhilarating. The Farm House came into view and

Juney races back to the Farm

Sam slowed, the road, just beyond the Farm was filled with Hare's, there must have been twenty, perhaps thirty.

"A 'drove' of Hares!" Sam said to herself, remembering her school lesson and the word for a group of Hares, *what an amazing sight,* she thought.

Chapter Six
Hare Today, Gone Tomorrow

Juney raced back to the Farm, the little girl following, and the red thing not far behind. She didn't really have a plan, just the thought that Human's would have control over the Hound, and the kind Farmer would hopefully free Freddy.

All the Jacks where there, and even a few of the Does. Tufty moved towards her and so did Harry and Billy.

"What are you doing, Juney?" Harry asked. He was watching the little girl nervously.

"I got Farmer and his family to follow me, I hope Farmer will free, Freddy," she replied. She was watching the Hound as she spoke; it was becoming very agitated by the presence of so many Hares.

"Grey Hound is angry," Tufty said needlessly.

By this time the little girl had found Freddy, and was trying to free him, but Freddy was screaming, a high-pitched wail, at her every touch and that noise was driving the Hound insane.

Farmer arrived and got out of the red thing, he walked over to Sam, and bent to help her. The Hares, with the exception of Juney and Tufty backed slowly away. Juney bounded across to sit next to Sam and spoke to a frantic Freddy, "FREDDY! It's me, Juney, the humans are here to help, stop struggling and let them hold you! They won't hurt you,"

she told him sternly. Freddy still moaned, but he
stilled and allowed the hands to touch him.

And then the Hound broke loose and hurtled
towards Freddy and Juney.

Grey Hound breaks free!

Sam was astounded when the blue-eyed Hare came across and sat beside her. She'd found the Hare caught in the hedge and seen the greyhound, and being an intelligent girl, she had figured out what was wrong. They still coursed Hares a couple of times a year at the Village Fete's and Sam detested it, but she knew, of all the dogs, greyhounds were the quickest and likeliest to catch a Hare.

Her Pa knelt beside her and said, "In all my years, I've never seen anything like this! Look at all those Hares!"

"It's really stuck, Pa," Sam said. She could see now, the fat Hare seemed calmed by the presence of the brown-toed Hare.

The greyhound was making a terrible racket and tore itself free, and to this day, Sam still had to shake herself and remind herself that she had actually seen what happened. The greyhound charged across the road, Adam jumped out of the car, and the blue-eyed Hare leapt into the air, spinning around, pulled back her powerful back legs and smashed her feet into the greyhound's snout, unbalancing it. The other Hare, with the odd tuft of hair between its ears, followed blue-eyes' example and slammed his big feet into the side of the teetering hound. And then Adam and her Pa shooed the hound away. Adam chased it for a good hundred yards up the road, away from the Hares.

Pa then went into the house and got a saw, and then he used it to free the trapped Hare, all the while the blue-eyed Hare and the one with the tufty hair, sat beside Sam and kept the fat Hare calm.

Freddy was free! He shook himself and ran up the road towards the rest of the Hares, who were all still there watching. The little girl reached out a hand and touched Tufty; the Jack leapt about six feet into the air and ran off. Juney stayed still and the girl gently stroked her head, it was not an unpleasant feeling and Juney didn't know what else to do to say thank you.

"You are a beauty," said the girl, though Juney didn't understand.

Farmer leaned down and stroked her too, and then she loped away. When she was amongst the rest of the Hares she turned. The little girl, and the other three Humans were watching and the little girl was waving.

Freddy was still befuddled, and mumbling to himself, "Thank you Lepus! I'll never say anything naughty about you again!"

"Well done, Juney," Tufty appeared at her shoulder.

"Well done you, Tufty, you were very brave, today," she told him.

Tufty smiled, "How do we say thank you to the Humans?" he asked.

Juney thought for a moment and then thumped her hind foot on the ground, Tufty did too, and then the rest of the Hare's started drumming. Juney kept the drumming up for a few moments and then she ran off into the lower farm field, and the Hares followed.

"Right, Juney Brown Toes, I'll race you up to High Meadow," Harry said, and he took off almost before he'd stopped talking.

Juney looked once, but she couldn't see the little girl anymore, and so she turned and hurtled after Harry, "This is how this all started earlier!" she said to herself, but she would not be beaten.

"Well as I live and breathe," Pa said, "I don't think any of the lads down the pub will believe a word of it!"

The drumming Hares had all gone now and Sam was feeling a bit sad. Her Mum gave her a big hug and said, "Well done, Sam. Come in the house and help me make tea."

With one last wistful look, Sam followed her family into the Farm House.

Hare Epilogue

"Well –I –understand –some –valuable –lessons –were –learned –today," said Wimble Whitecoat, sitting at the head of the night class.

Juney spoke up, "Yes, Wimble, we learned that not all Humans are bad, Farmer and the little girl helped to save Freddy. And I learned that the Grey

Hound, although fast, can be beaten with difficulty, but it is *best* avoided! I also learned all dogs are very dangerous to Hares, and 'The Hare of a Dog' is not a good game to play."

"I learned that Juney Brown Toes is the most smartest Hare that ever lived," Tufty said.

"And, Tufty Thomas is just about the bravest Jack I've ever known," Juney said.

"And I learned that, Juney Brown Toes is not unbeatable," said Harry smugly.

"We'll do the same race tomorrow, Harry. Only this time you don't get a head start, or take a short cut, or have another Jack bump into me, Ok?" Juney smiled innocently, and Harry sank into his Form in shame.

"And I learned that a Hare's breadth maybe does matter, and that I'd better eat less mushrooms, oh dear, oh dear!" Freddy moaned.

Epilogue
More Stories?

"So it was a true story, Mummy?" Patrick said, yawning.

"You're tired, Darling, time for an afternoon nap," Samantha replied.

"Tell me!"

"Well, everything outside the Farm House actually happened, the rest I made up, though we did find a dead Hare in the lower field, and our old Labrador seemed awfully tired that evening. So I like to think that most of it is true, although really it was just a little girl's imagination trying to make sense of a wondrous day," Samantha closed up the papers as she spoke and then stood, picking Patrick up.

"Are there any more stories, Mummy?" Patrick asked eagerly, "About the Hares?"

"You're getting too big to carry, Patrick," Samantha pretended to huff and puff as she carried him to his room.

"Patrick giggled, but insisted, "Are there any more stories about Hares?"

"There might be," Samantha said, "for good little boys, who go to sleep when they are supposed to."

Patrick turned over quickly and pretended to sleep. She stayed with him until he was really asleep and then she went to her room and pulled the suitcase from under the bed again. She opened it and took out a few bits of clothing, to reveal hundreds of pages of roughly written words, "I never will forget Juney Brown Toes, or that day, and oh yes, Patrick, there are so many more stories," Samantha said quietly to herself. She took out a few of the pages, closed her eyes for a moment, remembering, and then smiled as she began to read.

Juney Brown Toes

Wimble Whitecoat

Tufty Thomas

Freddy

Marty Flop Ear

Bobby